STRENGTH OF THE BEAST

TAROT FANTASIES SERIES

BOOK TWO

JAX WILDER

STRENGTH OF THE BEAST

Tarot Fantasies Series
Jax Wilder

RAINBOW QUARTZ PUBLISHING

Strength of the Beast© 2024 by Jax Wilder

Published by Rainbow Quartz Publishing

Edmonds WA, 98026

ISBN: 978-1-961714-46-5

First Edition: 2024

Cover design by Miranda Townsend

Interior design by Miranda Townsend

Tarot Card description by Lorelai Hamilton from the book Teenage Tarot – used with permission.

For permissions or inquiries, please contact:

Rainbow Quartz Publishing

rainbowquartzpublishing@gmail.com

RQPublishing.com

For every person who desired the Beast.

Jax Wilder

8. STRENGTH

"Courage is not the absence of fear. It's deciding that someone or something is more important than your fear, and doing it anyway," Strength.
Courage and bravery
Overcoming challenges with grace
Taming inner demons
Compassion and gentleness
Asserting control through patience
Self-confidence and self-belief
Triumphing over adversity
Embracing one's wild nature
Power from within

The Strength card is all about inner strength and bravery. You have the same power inside of you to face whatever challenges come your way. It's a reminder that you are so much stronger than you realize.

The Strength card isn't about being tough or aggressive. It's about being gentle and patient, even in the face of adversity. You don't have to fight fire with fire. Sometimes, a soft touch is all it takes.

—Lorelai Hamilton, author of *Teenage Tarot* and *Tarot Tales & Magic Spells*

VIII

STRENGTH.

ONE

With a delicate touch, I handled the anxious beagle on the exam table. "It's okay, buddy. Just a quick check-up, and you'll be back to chasing squirrels in no time." His tail wagged nervously through his whimpers. I scratched behind his ears, and he relaxed under my touch.

"You're amazing with him, Mia," Dr. Greene said. "I don't know how you do it."

Underneath the smile I wore, a flicker of doubt lingered. "It's just practice and a lot of patience."

"Since you've got this," he said before leaving, "I'm going to check on the Golden Retriever from today's surgery."

I finished the exam and sent the beagle back to his owner with a reassuring pat. As I cleaned up, the clinic door chimed, signaling another arrival.

I looked up and smiled. "Fancy seeing you here. What's in the box, girly?"

"Mia, you won't believe what I found!" Lea cried, hurrying over. I've known Lea for years. She's a well-known figure in this town, and everyone knows her as the owner of the beloved local bookstore, Spellbound Stories.

"Is it the books I ordered on the Rhyacotriton olympicus?"

"The what?"

"Salamanders," I giggled. I peeked into the box and gasped. "A baby raccoon! Where did you find him?"

"He was all alone near the park. Poor baby, I couldn't just leave him there. I wanted to make sure he's healthy and safe," Lea explained, her eyes wide with concern.

"Be honest. Did you want a pet raccoon?" I asked with a raised brow.

"You know I do, but he was all alone, and there were children nearby. What if he got hurt? What if they stepped on him? It didn't feel right leaving him there, with those monstrous children running around."

"Keep telling yourself whatever makes you sleep at night," I said with a wink. With great care, I lifted the tiny raccoon out of the box, feeling its delicate weight in my hands. He hissed at me, crouched down, claws out. Poor little dude was terrified. "You're a tough little guy, aren't you? He's adorable. Let's take a closer look at you, buddy."

The baby raccoon wriggled in my hands. I held him securely against my chest, giving him time to calm down, my movements practiced and gentle. I looked in his mouth and gave him a physical exam. "He's a bit dehydrated, but otherwise, he seems fine. You'll need to keep him warm and feed him formula every few hours."

Lea nodded eagerly. "I can do that. I can take care of him until he's a little older. Maybe later we can talk about how to reintroduce him to the wild. What else do I need to know?"

"If your husband is going to let you bring home a raccoon," I chuckled.

"Oh, you know Alex. He has permanent Christmas cheer, so I'll spin this as an early gift, and he won't be able to say no." Lea radiated joy looking at this little masked angel.

I handed her a list of instructions. "Here's everything you need. Make sure to follow the feeding schedule, and if he shows any signs of distress, bring him back immediately. You can schedule a follow-up at the front desk, and we'll get him his shots."

Lea grinned. "Thanks, Mia. You're so good with the little beasts. Speaking of which, have you heard about The Arcane Room?"

I shook my head. "The Arcane Room? I've heard of it but never been."

"It's this mystical shop in town. I think it might be just what you need. I have a sixth sense about these things, you know," Lea said.

"So, you say," I said, raising an eyebrow skeptically.

"You've been visibly tense and on edge lately, haven't you?"

"I mean, you're not wrong. But so is everyone else."

"When is the last time you got laid?"

"Lea!" I felt my cheeks flush.

"What? I'm just saying, I can tell it's been a while. Right?"

"Maybe…"

"I don't know, but there's something special about The Arcane Room. It has a way of adding a bit of brightness to your life. I think it could help you explore your wild side," Lea said with a mischievous glint in her eye.

I laughed softly. "My wild side? I'm not sure I have one."

"You'd be surprised," she insisted, a glimmer of mischief in her eyes. "I'll make an appointment for you. Go by after work and let them know I sent you. Consider it a thank you gift for looking after Renfield."

I shook my head. "Renfield? You've already named this little baby?"

She smiled a toothy grin.

"You're still going to set him free again, right? When he's old enough?"

She looked away, nodding a slow agreement.

"I'll talk to Alex about the severity of taking on a wild animal as a pet," I warned. "But if you can make it a positive thing, that would be best."

Laughter burst from me. "Sure, sure. I'll tell you

what, you have Alex call me about Renfield, and I guess I can give The Arcane Room a try. It's not like it can hurt."

"Exactly. There's only pain if you're into that kind of thing."

"What?"

Standing outside of The Arcane Room, I couldn't help but feel awkward. I'd seen the shop in town. It had an unassuming exterior with a simple wooden sign, but something about it always made me nervous. Like I wasn't cool enough to belong, let alone shop there.

Who was I? I was just Mia. That place was a sensory feast. Energy pulsed off it. Walking by the store, you couldn't help but feel drawn in.

Damn it, Lea… I pushed open the door, and the rich scent of incense enveloped me. The walls were adorned with a colorful array of books on magic, tarot cards, and shelves brimming with crystals and other enchanting objects. It was enchanting.

"Welcome," a silky velvet voice greeted me.

The woman behind the counter had long, dark hair and intricate tattoos adorning her arms. She was a striking figure. "I'm Ms. Vesper. Can I assist you in finding anything?"

Nerves fluttered in my stomach. "Nice to meet you, I'm Mia," I waved. "My friend suggested I come by. She said it might help me—explore my wild side?" I said, sounding more doubtful than I intended.

Ms. Vesper's eyes twinkled with understanding. "Ah, I see. You must be Lea's friend. She's a regular customer around here."

"Yeah, that checks," I laughed, glancing around the shop. "It smells delightful in here, by the way."

"Thank you," she said with a grin. "It's all part of the mystique."

"So, what things do you have going on here? I know Lea was a bit vague, but I was hoping you could shed some light on what she was referring to."

"We offer unique experiences here at The Arcane Room, guided by the power of tarot," Ms. Vesper said. "No two experiences are the same. But every one of them awakens something deep and carnal inside. Would you like to give it a try?"

The word "carnal" has always conjured an image of two people fucking like it's their last day on earth. I gulped. "I think Lea might kill me if I don't. But I'd like to know what to expect."

Ms. Vesper brought out a deck of tarot cards, their corners frayed and colors faded from years of use. She shuffled them. "Think about your deepest desires. It's different for everyone. Some people want love, others adventure. Whatever it is—you don't have to tell me—simply hold that feeling in your heart. I want you to feel it in your bones, and when you're ready, draw a card."

Closing my eyes, I took a deep breath. My deepest desire? I wasn't sure what that was. I have a good job, a good life really. Lea's words struck a chord within me, revealing a desire I wasn't ready to acknowledge—I yearned for something greater. I reached out and drew a card, handing it to Ms. Vesper.

"Strength," she said, her voice filled with admiration, as she showed me the card depicting a woman cradling a majestic lion. "This is a powerful card. Do you see how gentle she is with the lion? Anyone else would stand there in fear, but here she is, looking radiant, with her head right at his mouth. It's a symbol of courage, determination, and inner strength. Sometimes fear prevents us from living life. The Strength card says there's something more important than your fear." Ms. Vesper poured a cup of tea while she spoke. "This experience is immersive. It will open your heart to things you've craved."

"Okay," I said, hesitantly.

"If you can just sign this waiver, we'll get started," she said, sliding a document to me.

I signed without reading it.

"Follow me." Her voice was breathy, and I couldn't help but trust her. Ms. Vesper led me to a back room. When I entered, the room was almost blinding white. In the center was a leather chaise lounge.

"Have a seat and get comfortable." She handed me a cup of tea. "Drink this. It will help you relax into the experience."

I took the cup, smelling it before drinking. The tea was warm and soothing and carried floral notes. A sense of calm washed over me as I settled on the couch.

"No matter how much time passes in the simulation, only twenty minutes will have passed here. It could feel like hours or maybe days, and it won't apply here in this world. The important thing is to let yourself enjoy all of it." Ms. Vesper said, patting my arm. "In shadows deep where secrets dwell, I cast the Strength card's potent spell. Release what binds, set free your soul's embrace. By moonlight's grace, magic takes its place."

I closed my eyes, and when I opened them again, I was no longer in the cozy shop. Instead, I was standing in a dense, enchanted forest, the air thick with the scent of pine and moss. The trees towered above me, their leaves whispering secrets of things unseen.

Without warning, the tranquil forest was disrupted by the ominous sound of a low growl.

Adrenaline coursed through my veins as my heart pounded against my ribcage. I whirled around, my senses heightened as I tried to pinpoint the source of the noise. Cautiously, I took a step forward, holding my breath.

Another earth-shattering growl echoed through the air, causing the ground to tremble beneath my feet. As I strained my ears, I realized that whatever it was, it was now dangerously close.

I swallowed hard, steeling myself for whatever lay ahead.

Two

My heart threatened to leave my chest completely as I took a careful step toward the noise. Something was hurt, and I was still a doctor. I took an oath, and I wasn't about to let fear get the better of me.

With each passing moment, the snarl in the woods grew louder and more ominous, its menacing and hair-raising sound resonating deeply within the towering trees, causing an uncontrollable shudder to ripple down my spine. I scanned the forest, my eyes darting from tree to tree, hoping to glimpse its source. Peering through the dense foliage, I saw him.

A hulking beast emerged, its muscles flexing beneath a thick coat of fur, its eyes burning with a fierce intensity. He stood before me, an extraordinary mix of man and beast, unlike anything I had ever encountered. The combination of musk, cloves, and a faint trace of pine lingered in the air around him.

Moving with a predatory grace, he couldn't conceal the slight wince that accompanied each step.

He let out another howl, the sound resonating deep within me and causing heat to warm my belly. "Who are you?" he snarled, his voice rough and gravelly, yet undeniably human.

I took a deep breath, trying to steady my trembling hands. "My name is Mia. You're injured. Let me help you."

As his eyes narrowed, a fierce intensity flickered within them. He slowly revealed his teeth. It was a threatening display. "Stay back. I don't need your help."

Disregarding his caution, I inched closer, my gaze locked onto the bloodied wound in his side. It was horrifying. It looked like someone had stabbed him. The wound was deep and angry, blood trickled down his leg. "You're injured. You can't heal that on your own."

He snarled again, taking a step away. "I said stay back!"

I faltered, doubt creeping in. What was I thinking? This was a magical world, filled with dangers I couldn't possibly understand. Maybe this wasn't my calling.

His eyes held a deep pain that struck me, and in that moment, a powerful surge of determination coursed through my veins. "I can help you," I said, my voice shaking but firm. "Please, let me help."

He growled again, but this time, it sounded more

like frustration than anger. "Why should I trust you?"

"I'm a veterinarian," I replied without thinking. "Not that you're an animal. I wouldn't assume to know what you are, I—" I was babbling. Deep breath. "I'm a doctor. And because I want to help. I can't just leave you like this."

He watched me for a moment, his eyes searching mine. Then, with a reluctant sigh, he lowered himself to the ground. "Fine." Even as low as he was, I still had to reach to his wound. He was easily seven and a half feet tall. Maybe more.

Despite my efforts to calm my nerves, my hands were still trembling uncontrollably. "This might hurt a little, but I promise I'll be as gentle as I can."

He grunted in response, and I took that as permission to proceed. I inspected the wound more closely. It was deep, but not life-threatening. "What happened?" I asked, trying to keep him talking to distract him from the pain I was about to induce.

"Bandits," he replied, his voice tight with agony. "They ambushed me. I fought them off, but not before one of them got a lucky strike."

"I'm sorry," I mumbled. With a fanny pack slung across my chest and a tool belt secured around my waist, apparently, I was ready for anything. With urgency, I sifted through them, hoping to find supplies that would prove useful in this moment. I found a flask with water, a suture kit, and bandages. With great care, I cleaned the wound, ensuring that I removed any unwanted particles with precision. "I'm going to need to stitch this up."

He nodded, his jaw clenched. "Do what you have to."

My hands had been shaking, but I forced myself to focus and fall into a familiar rhythm. I worked quickly, my hands moving swiftly as I skillfully utilized the supplies. "What's your name?" I asked, trying to keep him distracted.

"Ezra," he growled.

"It's nice to meet you, Ezra. I'm Mia," I said, threading the needle. "I'm a healer."

He huffed. "I suppose that makes sense. You have a gentle touch."

With a smile on my lips, I could feel my confidence growing. "Thank you. I just need to finish stitching this up, and then I'll bandage it."

As he nodded, his intense, dark eyes stayed fixed on me. "Why are you here, Mia? This forest is no place for someone like you."

"I—I'm not sure," I admitted. "There was an inexplicable pull that drew me to this place. Maybe it was to help you." The transition to this world was still hazy in my mind. Everything felt so real, so vivid. My life felt like the dream. The entire experience was so immersive that it felt like stepping into another world. None of this was what I expected when I left work today.

Ezra's eyes briefly softened, a fleeting moment of tenderness that vanished in an instant. "You shouldn't be here. It's dangerous."

"I can handle it," I said, more to convince myself than him. "You're not the only one who needs help."

There was a pause, and then he released a heavy sigh, his emotions palpable. "Few would be brave enough to do what you're doing."

I finished stitching the wound and wrapped a bandage around his side. "There. That should hold for now. But you need to rest and let it heal."

"Why do you care so much, Mia?" Ezra asked.

I hesitated, thinking about my life back home, about the animals I cared for and the people I tried to help. "Because I can't stand to see anyone in pain. And because I believe everyone deserves a chance to heal."

Ezra's expression softened, and for a moment, I saw the man behind the beast. "Thank you," he breathed.

I smiled, feeling a strange sense of connection with this mysterious, tormented creature.

As I looked into his eyes, I felt a flicker of hope. Maybe I was stronger than I thought.

THREE

E zra was in excruciating pain. I'd just performed minor surgery in the middle of the forest, and I'm pretty sure I've lost my mind. I turned to him. "Is there somewhere safe you can go to rest, clean your wound, and heal?"

Ezra's eyes bore into mine, filled with desperation. "I can't heal it on my own."

The weight of his unspoken question settled over me. "Ezra, I'm just an ordinary veterinarian, not a superhero. You need a proper doctor."

"Please," he said, his voice breaking. "It's difficult to find healers in this area, and the nearest one is a hundred miles on foot. Besides, no one would help a beast."

There was something in his voice, a vulnerability that I couldn't ignore. "Alright," I breathed. "I'll stay and help. But I'm only here to help with your wound, nothing more."

With a simple nod, he conveyed his agreement. "Thank you, Mia."

My eyes scanned the dark forest, taking in the towering trees and the mysterious shadows that danced between them. "You need a place to rest. Is there somewhere safe we can go?"

Uncertainty flickered in Ezra's eyes before he finally nodded. "Yes. My home is nearby. It's not much, but it's safe."

"Lead the way," I said, trying to sound braver than I felt.

As we walked, I couldn't help but feel a mix of curiosity and fear. What was I getting myself into? Following a beast three times my size to a secluded location? I couldn't help but feel small compared to his impressively large muscles. Not to mention, I'm pretty sure he could crush me with his hands alone. It seemed insane. Despite my trepidation, there was an undeniable magnetism to Ezra that compelled me to help him.

Finally, after a long journey through the dense forest, we discovered a castle tucked away. Its ancient stones seemed to whisper of a strange and magical past. It was cold, dark, and damp, with an air of desolation. The massive steel doors opened on their own at Ezra's approach, creaking ominously.

"This is your home?" I asked, trying to hide my unease.

"It's not much, but you'll be safe."

We stepped inside, and I heard the faint scampering of footsteps. Candles lit themselves along the walls and filled the space with glowing light.

"Who else is here?" I asked, glancing around.

"No one to worry yourself about. They won't bother you," he said.

I nodded, though I still felt a little uneasy. "You should rest. Let me take care of that wound."

Leading me through the corridors, Ezra brought me to a sizable dining hall. A massive wood table dominated the room, flanked by a dozen towering high-back chairs. "Would you like some dinner?" he asked.

"We should clean the wound first."

"It can wait, but my hunger won't." Ezra looked at me as if he wanted to eat me.

For a moment, I think I might have let him. My stomach growled in response. "Okay. But I'm giving you a full examination after."

Ezra huffed, "If you insist."

"I do."

He motioned to a chair. "Please, have a seat."

From across the table, I could feel the tension in the air as we locked eyes. To my astonishment, our first course, three hors d'oeuvres each, magically appeared before us. It appeared to be dates stuffed with goat cheese and cold-smoked salmon, with a thin line of honey on top.

I took one into my mouth. The complex combination of sweet and savory was delectable.

"Do you like it?" he asked.

"Mmm," I mumbled through a full bite. I swallowed. "I've never had anything so rich and creamy. It's delicious." When we finished the last of the dates, the plates disappeared just as mysteriously as they arrived.

The next course was a caprese salad. The mozzarella was next level. "Who's your chef?" I asked, genuinely wondering how such delectable foods could come from a castle as cold as this one and so far from society.

"They've been with me for as long as I can remember," Ezra said. "I will pass your affections along. Now, tell me something about yourself." His words did not feel like a request.

"Umm," I cleared my throat, searching for the right words to placate this beast. "I've always had a fondness for animals. That's the reason I pursued a career in veterinary medicine - dealing with people can be tough, but working with animals is easy. Sometimes I prefer easy. Especially the fuzzy and cuddly ones," I admitted with a smile.

A deep, rich chuckle escaped Ezra's lips, unexpectedly sending warmth through the space between my legs. "I'm a bit fuzzy," he said, eyes heating with an intensity that only turned me on more. "And I can be quite cuddly."

Desire surged through me, making my cheeks turn rosy. "I suppose you are," I said.

The next course populated at the table.

I ignored it.

Despite the strangeness of the situation, there was an odd sense of warmth in Ezra's company. There was something about him that made me feel safe, as if his presence could ward off the eerie silence that filled the dark, mysterious castle.

As the evening went on, we continued to talk, and I found myself growing more and more drawn to him. Despite his beastly appearance, there was a gentleness and vulnerability in Ezra that I couldn't resist.

He was laughing again. "A raccoon, as a pet?" Ezra wiped a tear away. "That would be like saying I wanted to have you as a pet."

His words brought me up short. The idea of being his pet was more appealing than I was comfortable with. He could pet me, brush my hair, and take me on walks. Then after I've been a good girl, I could lie in his lap while he strokes my back.

"I think it's time you got some rest," I said finally, trying to ignore the raw carnality of my feelings. "You need to heal."

Ezra nodded and stood. "You're right."

I watched as he left the dining hall, my mind racing with a thousand thoughts. What had I gotten myself into? And why did I feel this intense pull toward him, despite everything?

As I wandered through the castle and prepared to find a place to sleep, Ezra was waiting for me at the top of the stairs. "Mia?"

"Yes?"

"You said you would be giving me a full examination after dinner."

"I did say that, didn't I."

"It's after dinner now."

Four

E zra waited for me to climb the grand staircase, then led me down several dark and musty passageways until we stopped at a room with double wood doors.

"This is me," he said.

"Should I—we—I mean, should I come in?" I rambled, my nerves betraying me.

"Yes, I think it will be more comfortable in here."

He led me inside, where I found the dimly lit room was spacious and yet surprisingly cozy. The walls were lined with rich mahogany paneling, and tapestries depicting forest-like scenes adorned the walls. A large, four-poster bed dominated the center of the room, its dark, intricately carved wood standing in stark contrast to the crimson and gold bedding. The bed looked inviting and soft, with an abundance of pillows.

To the right, there was a stone fireplace, its flames flickering warmly, casting a soft glow over the room.

Opposite the bed, a large arched window framed by heavy velvet curtains looked out into the dark night. A few plush chairs were arranged around a low table, and a bookshelf overflowing with volumes stood against one wall. The room smelled faintly of pine and musk, a scent that seemed to be a natural part of Ezra.

Ezra moved with a grace that belied his size, settling himself on the edge of the bed with a wince. "I think I need your help now, Mia," he said, his voice gravelly.

I wondered if he could hear my heart pounding in my chest. The last time I felt this nervous vomited. I took a deep breath, trying to steady myself. "Let's get you out of those pants so I can tend to your wound properly."

My fingers trembled slightly as I undid the laces of his trousers. He wore no shirt, his broad, hairy chest and muscular arms exposed, the firelight dancing along his body. As I pulled his pants down, I couldn't help but notice the sheer size and strength of his thighs, the powerful muscles beneath the skin. This was nothing like treating an injured dog or cat; this was a living, breathing myth.

I tried not to stare at his manhood. He wasn't erect, and I already feared how big he'd grow when aroused.

Once his pants were off, I could clearly see the extent of his injury. The bandage I applied earlier in the forest was soaked through with blood. I carefully removed it, my fingers brushing against his flesh, feeling the warmth of his body. He watched me fixedly, his gaze burning with an intensity that made my cheeks flush and my heart pulse.

An unseen servant had left out a tray with a bowl of water, clean cloths, and a jar of ointment. I soaked a cloth in the water and began to gently clean the wound. As I worked, I couldn't help but notice how close we were. His breath was hot on my neck, and his body radiated heat. I'm pretty sure his hands are so large they could easily crush me. My ex used to have a temper, but Ezra's presence felt different—there was a gentleness beneath his rough exterior.

But instead of fear, I felt a strange exhilaration. There was something undeniably attractive about his beastly nature, the raw power and strength that seemed to emanate from him. I found myself drawn to him, my body reacting to his presence in a way that I couldn't ignore. It was a feeling I hadn't allowed myself to experience in years, not since my last relationship ended in heartbreak.

"Thank you, Mia," Ezra said, his voice low, taking on a husky quality.

I smiled, my hands stilling for a moment. "Just doing my job," I breathed. I finished cleaning the wound and applied the ointment, my fingers lingering on his skin a little longer than necessary. The contact sent a thrill through me, and I could feel his eyes on me, tracing my every move.

Ezra's hands were twice the size of my head, large and strong. He reached out and stroked my hair, his fingers tangling in the strands. "You're very brave, Mia," he murmured.

My breath caught in my chest, warmth pooling in my cunt. "Ezra…" I began, but he cut me off, his eyes darkening with desire.

"I want you, Mia," he said, his voice liquid with need. "I've wanted you every second since I first laid eyes on you."

Before I could respond, he reached out and pulled me closer, his hands rough on my clothes but still gentle on my body. He tore at my top, ripping it off me, shredding it in the process. Baring his teeth, Ezra moved like he was going to bite my neck, only instead he tore my bra into pieces, leaving my breasts exposed.

He tilted his head, watching me, waiting for a reaction. My nipples hardened, breasts aching for his touch. If he touched me right then, I might have died from arousal.

Ezra motioned me forward with a playful wiggle of his finger.

I obeyed without words.

"Good girl." He slid two fingers into my pants and ripped them off me as well. I stepped out of them, and Ezra tossed them aside.

The suddenness of it took my breath away, and I found myself trembling again. Not with fear this time, but with anticipation.

I was completely naked, feeling exposed and vulnerable in his presence.

Ezra slid back into the bed, and I noticed just

how aroused he was as well. His cock was thick and wet with pre-cum. "Come to me," he commanded, his voice low and authoritative. "I'm going to fuck you."

I crawled up onto the bed, feeling the softness of the mattress beneath me. The bed was tall, and I had to literally climb up, my movements slow and deliberate. Ezra's gaze locked onto me, his eyes brimming with hunger and anticipation.

As I got closer to him, he reached out and grabbed my hips, pulling me onto his lap. I could feel his hardness pressing against me, and a gasp escaped my lips. His size was so immense that I questioned whether he could actually fit.

Ezra positioned me on top of him, his hands guiding me as I slowly lowered myself onto his member. I took him inside of me, one inch at a time.

As the feeling grew stronger, I couldn't help but hold my breath, the intensity almost too much to handle. I cried out, whimpering as my center expanded to take him into me. My body reacted instinctively to his.

I moved slowly at first, Ezra lifting my hips then bringing me down to meet him again. Faster this time, finding the rhythm between our bodies. I was riding him with a growing intensity. Ezra's hands gripped my hips, his fingers digging into my flesh as he matched my movements.

The rhythmic pumping of his cock, his hands caressing my skin, it was an incredibly intense experience. Tension coiled inside me, heat rising, until I reached the pinnacle of pleasure. I cried out, my body rapture with release.

But Ezra wasn't done.

His mouth found mine in a passionate kiss before he pulled out of me. I felt so empty without him inside me. His mouth moved across my body, licking and nipping a path over my skin with his teeth until I was practically sitting on his face.

Ezra parted my throbbing legs further and looked at my sex. He licked his lips before diving between my folds. He tasted my pussy, licking up my natural juices. With his nose pressed against my clit, he skillfully used his tongue to bring me to another intense climax.

He flipped me over, positioning me on my hands and knees. Ezra entered me again, his movements rougher this time, more urgent. He fucked me. I leaned into him, internally begging him to go deeper, to fuck me harder.

Then he did, until he erupted inside of me, filling me with his seed, reaching between us, and with one stroke of my clit, I came for a third time. The sensation was distinct, more intense. I cried out with each thrust. Screaming his name as he drove me to the edge and beyond. My body shuddered with each wave of pleasure.

I was breathless, my body quivering, as he finally pulled out of me, his eyes filled with a mix of desire and deep satisfaction.

Ezra gathered me in his arms, pulling me close to him. I could feel his heartbeat against my cheek, strong and steady. He stroked my hair, his fingers gentle and soothing. "Good girl," he whispered.

I felt a sense of peace wash over me, a contentment I hadn't felt in a long time. I cuddled against him, my body fitting perfectly against his. My eyes closing as exhaustion overtook me. In that moment, I thought about my lonely nights, the empty feeling I tried to fill with work.

He continued to stroke my hair and my back, his touch gentle and comforting. "Sleep, Mia," he said softly. "I'll keep you safe."

And with those words, I drifted off to sleep, feeling safe and satisfied in Ezra's arms. For the first time in a long while, I felt a sense of belonging, a feeling that maybe, just maybe, this strange turn of events was exactly what I needed to heal the wounds I had carried for so long.

FIVE

When I woke, the first thing I noticed was the warmth beside me, curled around my body, hot breath on my neck. I pulled him closer, but something was wrong. I opened my eyes, expecting to see the comforting form of the beast who had cradled me to sleep after the truly mind-blowing sex the night before. My heart skipped a beat as realization hit. This was not his arm. I rolled to see who it was, cuddling me all night. It was at that precise moment when our eyes met, and I found myself face to face with a complete stranger.

A scream erupted from me as I scrambled to the edge of the bed, pulling the covers around me as a shield. "Who are you?" I demanded, my voice shaking.

The man sat up slowly, his hands raised in a calming gesture. "Mia, please, it's me. Ezra," he said, voice filled with sincerity. "I promise, it's just me."

I blinked, trying to make sense of the transformation before me. The man standing in front of me now seemed worlds apart from the beast I had encountered just hours ago. This man was still tall and wide. His features were similar to Ezra's. He had a similar muscular build, complete with thick thighs, reminiscent of his counterpart, although he lacked the same profusion of body hair. His dark brown eyes were a constant amidst all the changes, their intensity never wavering.

"Ezra? But... you were..."

"A beast?" he finished for me.

I nodded. "You look so different." His voice was the same, and somehow he still soothed my aching soul.

"It was you, Mia. You broke the spell."

My eyes widened. "What spell?"

Ezra sighed, running a hand through his tousled brown hair. "A curse. It was placed on me many years ago." He had a far-off look in his eyes, remembering a past life he thought he'd never see again. "The years blur together. I hardly remember how long I've been trapped. That beastly form was a cage I couldn't break free from. I never thought..." he trailed off. "Until I met you."

My heart pounded even harder, the rush of adrenaline drowning out all other sounds. "Me? How could I have? How did I? I didn't break anything, though."

"Can't you see, Mia? You did. The curse could only be broken by someone who truly saw me for who I am, beyond the beastly exterior," Ezra explained. "Someone who cared for me despite my monstrous appearance. Your kindness, your bravery, it's what broke the spell."

My mind spun with the revelation. "But why didn't you tell me?"

"Would you have believed me?" he asked gently. "It was always something you had to come to on your own. No one ever got close enough to try breaking it, and I couldn't bring myself to coerce someone into attempting it. I've been alone for a long time."

I stared at him, taking in his features. He was handsome, with a strong, chiseled chin, and his piercing gaze seemed to penetrate deep into the depths of my soul.

There was a familiarity in his gaze that pulled at my heart, the ache threatening to pull me under. It was the same man, but how? "I don't know what to say."

"You don't have to say anything," Ezra said, cupping my cheek. "I understand this is a lot to take in. It's a lot for me, and I knew it might happen. When you refused to leave me outside to die."

"I could never," I said, disgusted at the thought of anyone hurting him. "What happens now? You're no longer trapped as a beast. I suppose that means the world is your proverbial oyster."

"I want you, Mia."

My thoughts raced at his words.

Ezra sat up taller and scooted closer to me. He

laced his fingers inside my own. "I want you to stay here with me, Mia. Be my wife. Be mine."

I removed my hands from his, shaking my head. "I've never wanted anything more in my whole life," tears threatened to prick my eyes. "But I can't," I whispered, my tears falling freely onto my cheeks. "I have to go back. This isn't my home. I can't. It's all temporary. I have a life in the real world. I can't stay. No matter how much I want to."

Ezra's eyes softened, a look of understanding and sadness crossing his features. "You broke my curse, Mia. Now, I will do whatever it takes to break yours."

My brow furrowed. "My curse?"

"The loneliness, the feeling of being lost. I can see it in your eyes," Ezra said, his voice earnest. "Stay with me, and we can build a life together."

I felt a lump forming in my throat as a sob threatened to escape. Torn between the life I knew and the one he was offering. "I don't know if it's even possible. I think when I have to go back, I just disappear."

Ezra leaned into me, his lips brushing against my forehead. "Let me show you how much I can care for you, how much I need you, one last time."

In an instant, he silenced any words I might have spoken by pressing his lips against mine, the kiss transforming from gentle to intense. His hands roamed my body, reacquainting themselves with every curve and contour. Despite my confusion and the overwhelming sadness, I felt at having to leave him, my body responded to his touch. I craved the connection we shared.

Ezra's touch was both comforting and electrifying, a blend of familiarity and something new. His hands explored me with a gentleness that belied the intensity of his desire. "I love you, Mia." With each tender word he spoke against my skin, he expressed his unwavering commitment to love me for the rest of his life, leaving no doubt about the future we would build together.

As we made love, I lost myself in Ezra, the world outside slipping away. His body was different, yet there was a sense of rightness in our union. The same girth of his manhood filled me, over and over, bringing me to the brink of ecstasy. I cried out his name as he drove me to climax, my body shuddering with the force of my release. Stars burst behind my eyes and I thought for the briefest moment—if this was all there was to life, if it was this man and this single moment to my life—what a perfect life it would be.

Ezra shuddered in my arms, the heat of his seed warming my insides. He held me close, nipping at my neck. We lay together in the aftermath, our bodies entwined, the bond between us stronger than before.

"I will find you again, Mia," Ezra whispered, his voice filled with conviction. "No matter where you go, I will come for you."

I held onto him, tears streaming down my face. "Promise me. Promise me you won't stop looking for me and I promise I won't stop looking for you."

With his lips gently touching mine in a final kiss, he whispered, "I promise I will never stop looking for you. I will find you, my love."

"Always?"

"Always."

As I closed my eyes, the world around me shifted. It was like riding in a boat with high waves. When I opened them again, I was back in the Arcane Room. The memories of my time with Ezra hit me like a truck.

It was real.

It was all so real.

Six

When I woke, I was back in the Arcane Room. The luxurious couch seemed almost surreal after the intensity of my time with Ezra.

Oh, Ezra…

My heart. How did this happen? I thought this was supposed to be relaxing, but now my heart hurt. A deep longing for Ezra coursed through my entire body.

Ms. Vesper was there to greet me when I woke, her serene smile a stark contrast to the turmoil inside me.

"Hello, Mia. How was it?" she asked gently, her eyes filled with an unknowable understanding.

I burst into tears, the weight of everything crashing down on me. "How did this happen?"

I felt the warmth of Ms. Vesper's presence as she sat beside me, her arm reaching around to caress my shoulder. There was something about her presence that brought a sense of comfort. "Sometimes the Arcane Room awakens parts of us we weren't prepared for," she said softly.

I wiped at my tears, feeling a hollow ache in my chest. "I loved him. I loved Ezra, and I can't remember if I told him. I have to find him, no matter what it takes." Another sob wracked my body. "Is there anything I can do to ease this overwhelming sense of emptiness and anguish within me?" I mumbled through tears.

Ms. Vesper offered me a handkerchief. "You have to hold on deep in your heart to the things we want in this world, Mia. Know that the experience you had was real. Whatever was meant to find you has already found you once, and it will find you again."

I nodded, comforted by her words but still struggling with the emptiness I felt. Ms. Vesper led me back into the main shop. "I have something for you. Just give me one moment." She glided to the crystal shelf and palmed something into her hand. Then she moved through the incense aisle, looking for something in particular. When she found it, she handed me a rose quartz and a bundle of two hundred and fifty pine-scented incense. "These are special," she said, her eyes twinkling. "They are one of a kind, and I can't promise we'll ever get them in stock again. They will help you remember, no matter how much time passes, it's only twenty minutes. So, use them wisely."

I wasn't entirely sure what she meant, but I thanked her and paid all the same. I just wanted to go home, to crawl into my bed and dream of Ezra.

Dream of my love.

As I stepped out of the Arcane Room and back into the real world, everything felt disorienting. It had not even been forty minutes since I left work, yet my mind felt exhausted, as if I had been through a week's worth of emotional rollercoaster.

In a daze, I mechanically walked to my car, barely registering the sounds of traffic or the feel of the pavement beneath my feet. Back at home, I made myself some dinner, the comforting clinks and sizzles of the kitchen providing a stark contrast to the profound emotions still lingering within me. Before dishing up a plate for myself, I lit one of the incense sticks from Ms. Vesper. I don't think I would have chosen pine for myself, but I trusted Ms. Vesper. No matter how much it sucked right now, I know what she did for me was magic.

The room filled with the scent of musk, cloves, and pine, the combination immediately reminding me of Ezra. It was the most intoxicating scent, almost as if he was there with me.

Inhaling deeply, I closed my eyes, allowing the intoxicating aroma and fond memories of him to wash over me. Just then, I felt a firm embrace from behind, as muscular arms enveloped my body. I opened my eyes to find Ezra standing behind me.

I spun around. "How did you...?" I stammered,

tears welling up in my eyes. "I don't understand. You were gone. I was here. I..."

Ezra's hand gently cupped my cheek, his touch grounding me. "It's magic, Mia. I told you I'd break your curse. I found a way to be with you again."

"How long will you be here?" I asked, my voice trembling with hope and fear.

"For the length of the incense," he replied with a shrug. "No matter how long I'm gone, only twenty minutes will have passed. This magic is a little beyond my understanding. Every passing second without you feels like a lost chance for happiness. I want you, Mia. I need you." Ezra breathed me in. "Come, let me make love to you."

I nodded enthusiastically, not caring about the logistics or the time we had. All that mattered was that he was here with me. I would not waste a single moment with Ezra. I'd never take life for granted again.

We moved to the bedroom, our hands exploring each other with a desperate urgency. The familiarity of his touch, now heightened by the knowledge that our time was limited, intensified every lingering sensation. Ezra's lips found mine, his hands mapping my body as if he was memorizing every inch.

He tore at my clothing, and I helped him remove my work scrubs. I couldn't move fast enough to remove his pants, feeling them slip off my fingers and land in a messy pile on the floor. I held him at arm's length, wanting to take in the sight of him fully naked, the most beautiful man I'd ever had the privilege of seeing, and in my home, no less. "You're still my beast."

Ezra growled, threw me over his shoulder, and deposited me on the bed. My hands instinctively reached for his cock, and I could feel its powerful pulsations beneath my touch. He slipped his hand between us, sliding it the length of me, until it found my center and he slipped a finger inside me. "You're dripping wet."

"This is what you do to me," I said through ragged breaths.

Ezra's seductive eyes locked onto mine. "I'm going to fuck you now," he said.

A mischievous giggle escaped my lips as he playfully pinned me down, his presence overwhelming as he entered me completely.

As we made love, the world outside ceased to exist. The only reality was us, together, sharing this moment. His touch was gentle yet possessive, a silent declaration of his ownership over me. With every movement he made, his desire consumed him. I responded to him with equal fervor, my body craving the connection we shared.

We climaxed together, our cries mingling as we reached the peak of ecstasy. The warmth of his seed filled me, and for a moment, everything was perfect. We lay together, panting, until our pulses calmed.

"Do you love this place?" he asked.

"I love you," I said.

"I know, my heart. But do you love this place, this home you've created for yourself?"

I nodded, wishing more than anything for him to stay. "Until I met you, it was the only home I'd ever known."

"Now, where is home?" Ezra asked.

"In your arms," I said, snuggling closer to him. The night stretched on, and we held each other tight, not wanting to let go until the break of dawn.

Ezra whispered into my ear, "I will find you again, Mia." His voice filled with conviction. "No matter where you go, I will come for you."

We kissed one last time, the promise of our love hanging in the air. As the incense burned down, a sense of peace and contentment settled into me. When the aroma finally faded, Ezra began to disappear, his form becoming translucent.

"Always?" I asked, my voice breaking.

"Always," he replied, his voice echoing as he vanished.

I closed my eyes, holding onto the memory of him. When I opened them again, I was alone, but the scent of pine and sex lingered, a reminder of our time together. I held the rose quartz close, knowing that whatever the future held, I had to believe in the magic of our love.

Sign up for Jax Wilder's newsletter and receive a collection of unpublished Coral Cove short stories. Meet familiar characters and dive deeper into the love and romance that Coral Cove is known for. Don't miss out on this exclusive content!

Jax Wilder

If You enjoyed Strength of the Beast
Check out the first book in the Coral Cove series by
Jax Wilder

A Steamy, Curvy Girl, Hidden Identity, Small Town, Holiday Romance

Lea:
Christmas spirit is alive and well and like every other holiday—sales are up. The only part of this time of year I do celebrate. Until the sexiest man I've ever seen saunters into my little bookshop and sprinkles holiday cheer of his own. When he asks me to go with him to watch the tree lighting, what starts as a meet cute, turns something sweet into something equally spicy.

Alex:

It was only supposed to be a night away from the North Pole. Just a little breather before the big day. But then I met the red headed, curvy goddess of my dreams. Can I convince her not only that Santa Claus is real, but that I'm the man who brings the magic of Christmas to life?

Also by Jax Wilder

Coral Cove Series

Sleighed by Love

Harvesting Love

Dawning Desire

Knead You Now

Love Rewound

Haunted by Her

Perfect Lover Spell

Tarot Fantasies Series

The Devil's Temptations

Strength of the Beast

Hanged Passions

Death's Embrace

Jax Wilder

Teenage Witch's Grimoire

Tarot Reflection Journal

Tarot Refection Journal Coloring The Tarot

The Eclectic Witch's Grimoire

Dream Journal

Teenage Tarot

Tarot Tales and Magic Spells

Arcane In Verse

Isla Watts

A Fairy Bad Day

Surprise! You're a Vampire

Gorgeous, Gorgeous, Gorgons

Mork The Handsome Orc

Adopted By Werewolves

Bite Me If You Can

That's The Spirit!

Rose Dawson's Book Journals

My Time With The Fairies

Enchanted Escapades

Enchanted Escapades

Dewey Decimal Diaries

Siren's Songbook

Pride and Prejudice

Bibliophile's Bounty

Book of Books Journal

Pages & Passages Reading Journal

Bookworm's Companion Reading Journal & Tracker

About the Author

Jax Wilder is a passionate romance author hailing from a charming small town nestled in the picturesque Pacific Northwest. With a heart full of love and an unyielding belief in the power of happily ever afters, Jax weaves enchanting tales of love and connection that leave readers captivated.

Jax's novels are a reflection of her commitment to celebrating the magic of love, and her characters' journeys mirror the warmth and happiness she has found in her own life. Join her on the enchanting journey of love, passion, and enduring connection through her heartfelt romance novels.

amazon.com/stores/Jax-Wilder/author/B0CM36CSH1?ref=ap_r dr&isDramIntegrated=true&shoppingPortalEnabled=true